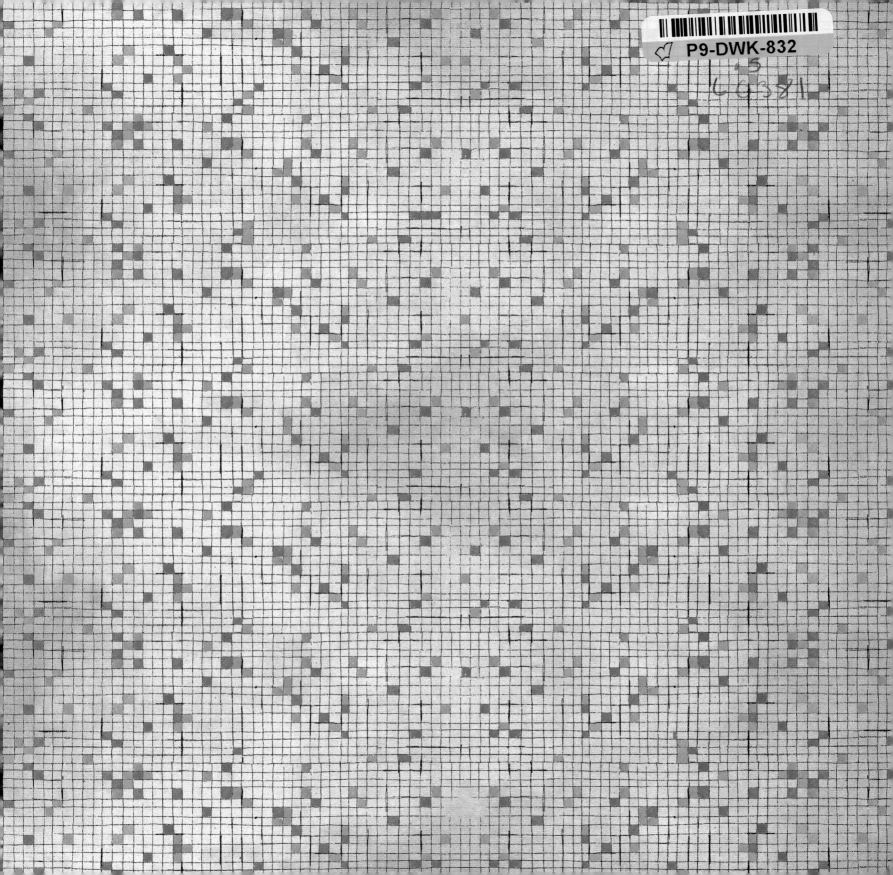

# A PIG NAMED

# PERRIER

Written by
**ELIZABETH SPURR**

Illustrated by
**MARTIN MATJE**

Hyperion Books for Children
New York

Printed in Hong Kong

First Edition
1 3 5 7 9 10 8 6 4 2

This book is set in 17-point Cochin.

Library of Congress Cataloging-in-Publication Data on file.
ISBN: 0-7868-0302-9
Visit www.hyperionchildrensbooks.com

*For the Breakfast Bunch*
—E.S.


*For my three little ones*
—M.M.

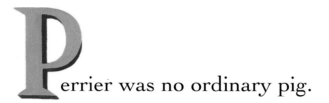errier was no ordinary pig.

He was a pedigreed miniature potbellied pig,
purchased from a Beverly Hills pet store by
Marbella, the rich and famous movie star.

Marbella treated Perrier like a prince. She settled him in a white satin bassinet in the nursery of her mansion—a place as posh as it was plush, and spic as it was span.

She gave Perrier a rhinestone-studded harness, a jaunty sports cap, and special piglet-sized dark glasses. A British nurse-nanny minded him while the actress was under studio lights.

Was he happy? Of course. Except for . . .

Except for what?

Perrier didn't know.

Marbella carried Perrier everywhere in her designer shoulder bag.

He was the toast of Hollywood parties.

"So bright and bubbly," chuckled his admirers.

"So round and cuddly."

"And so clean, so very *clean*!"

"Oh, yes." Marbella twinkled. "Unlike common pigs, potbellies are immaculate."

She nuzzled him, leaving lipstick on his ears.

Perrier loved the Hollywood life. He loved the canapés at parties, (except for cocktail sausages). He loved sitting in a booster chair at fashionable restaurants.

He loved being spied on by the paparazzi.

But in the midst of all the ritz and glitz, sometimes he felt a deep longing, a hankering in his hide, an emptiness in the pit of his little potbelly.

Something was missing.

# BUT WHAT?

One day Marbella said to him, "This Hollywood hoopla is driving me mad. We must get away to my country place."

The nurse-nanny packed Perrier's toys and bassinet, while Marbella's personal maid loaded the car with hatboxes and trunks.

"Give me the simple life!" sang Marbella, as the four of them roared down the road in her custom sports convertible.

Perrier enjoyed country living. Each day after his swim, he curled up on his pool lounge chair and breathed in new smells: earth and hay and blossoming orchards. His ears perked to new sounds: *baa*s and *cluck*s and *moo*s.

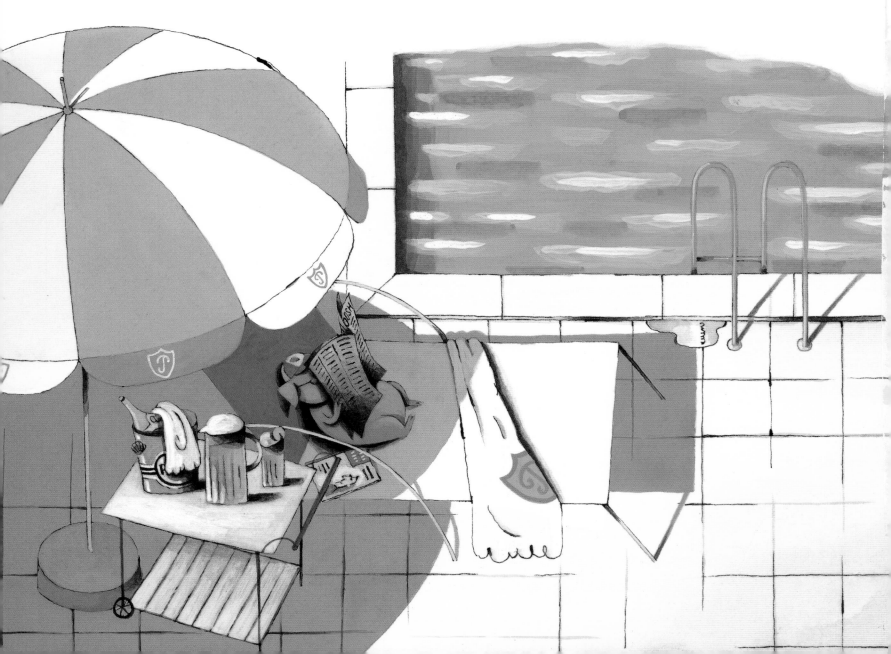

But one day came another sound. Perrier sat up. Drifting across the meadow came the music of squeals and *oink*s!

As his nurse-nanny dozed under the umbrella, Perrier crept off his lounge chair. Following the sounds, he gamboled across the fields to a nearby barnyard.

oink!
oink!

There he found a large sow with
six piglets, rolling and sloshing in
a puddle of thick, dark goo.
Perrier stared, pop-eyed.

"Eew! What *is* this?" he said.

"Our new swimming pool," said
the piglets. "Take a dive. The mud
is fine."

"*Mud?*" Perrier edged closer. "But
it's so sloppy and slimy."

"Good for what ails you," said the sow.
She shook and splattered him.

"Ma'am!" protested Perrier. The mud made
his hide tingle.

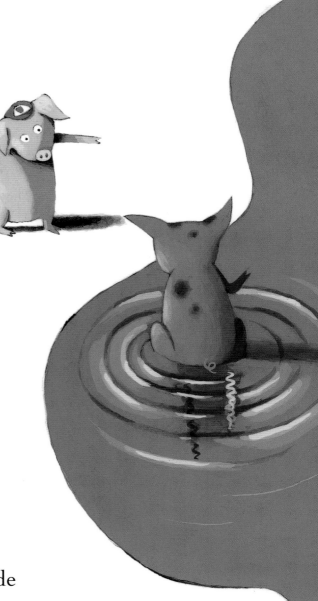

SPL

"Try it, you'll like it," giggled the pigs, as one of them gave him a shove.

# AT!

Perrier tumbled in, sports cap, glasses, and all.

*Mubble bubble*. Such a strange, slathery sensation. He felt . . .
that's it . . . *sensational!* His hide goose-bumped and tiddle-
lumped in delight.

Along with the piglets, he ished and squished, slushed and
mushed, mucked and mired, all the while humming, "Give me
the simple life!"

He completely forgot about Marbella until the sun dropped
behind the hills.

When Perrier got home, he knew he was late and in trouble. But Marbella would surely forgive him when she learned of his great discovery!

He peeked in the window. Marbella was stretched out on the sofa. Behind her stood the nurse-nanny, the personal maid, and the sheriff. A doctor hovered over her with a stethoscope. She was waving her hands and wailing, "Someone has kidnapped my baby!"

Much ashamed, the polluted pig skulked into the parlor, dripping mud on the white carpet.

"EEEE!" shrieked Marbella and fell into a faint.

While the doctor tended to Marbella, the nurse-nanny put on long rubber gloves and gave Perrier the bubble bath of his life. "My word, you're smirched clear through!" she grumbled, nearly scrubbing off his hide.

Then she wrapped him in a cashmere shawl and delivered him to his mistress, still moaning on the sofa. Marbella took the bundle in her arms. "Promise me you will never run away again!" Perrier hung his head.

"And that you will never *ever* again muddy yourself like a common pig!"

Perrier crossed his hooves over his heart.

Not long after that, Marbella put down the phone and swooped Perrier into her arms. "Baby, I'm making a new film. *Ooh la la*, in *Paris*!"

Perrier knew what that meant: no more of the simple life. Just as well. That mud pool and his wallowing friends were much too close for comfort.

Perrier had promised to stay clean.

Off they flew to visit the Eiffel Tower and the Arc de Triomphe.
Marbella replaced Perrier's cap with a beret.

The Parisian film directors huddled around him. "*Voilà, le porc*, how
pink and clean."

"Wee, wee," squeaked Perrier.

"*Quel* pig!" they exclaimed. "He even speaks *français*!"

After Paris, the two glittered at foreign
film festivals. Through all this high life,
Perrier felt restless and sad. He had
not been the same since his after-
noon in the luscious ooze, where
he had fulfilled his inner longing.
Try as he might, he could not
purge his urge to sludge.

Now he sat brooding on the beach of the Riviera. What fun were
pure white sand and clear blue water? He wanted muck! But Perrier
had promised to stay clean.

Fall came to California, then the winter rains. Perrier, in his new hand-knit sweater, stared out of the nursery window. Streams of water were making puddles in the garden—glistening, dark brown puddles. He could feel his hide crawl with anticipation. He turned from the window and wiped away a tear.

Perrier had promised to stay clean.

As the days passed, Perrier grew pale and listless. Marbella took him to the veterinarian, who prescribed warm baths every night. The once plump pig began to melt away.

Frantic over his condition, Marbella moved Perrier's bassinet to her bedroom. That night, thunder rumbled over Beverly Hills. A bolt of lightning flashed through the garden. Perrier whimpered.

Marbella jumped out of bed, turned on the light, and leaned over the bassinet. "It's okay, Baby. Mummy's here."

Perrier opened his eyes and stared up at her in disbelief. Her face! Her creamy white skin was covered with . . . Could it be?

It *was*. Her movie-perfect face was caked with scrumptious, chocolate-colored mud!

The next night, Perrier followed Marbella to her vanity table. She took off her eyelashes and washed off her makeup. Then she opened a jar and patted mud all over her face.

Perrier squealed and did a jig around the room.

"Whatever is the matter?" asked Marbella through her mask.

She took him into her arms. He nosed the mud; it rubbed off on his snout.

"Why, you little dear. You want some, too?"

She opened the jar and spread mud over Perrier's face.

His skin prickled with pleasure; he wriggled with joy.

That night, despite a raging storm, Perrier enjoyed the best sleep he'd had in months.

In the morning, Marbella sent her personal maid to buy several cases of Mother Earth's Secret. Each evening, she and Perrier shared their bedtime beauty ritual. He soon grew round and rosy again.

On Perrier's birthday, Marbella said, "I have a special treat for you." She drove him to a luxurious hot spring near Palm Desert—an exclusive celebrity hideaway.

And there the two of them, side by side, wallowed in mud baths from morning until night.